The Complete Hermeticism Philosophy Collection (Vol. 3)

*The Chaldean Oracles, Coelum Philosophorum &
The Emerald Tablet of Thoth — Oracular,
Alchemical & Cosmic Insights*

A Modern Translation

Adapted for the Contemporary Reader

Julian the Theurgist | Paracelsus
Hermes Trismegistus

Translated by Tim Zengerink

Table of Contents

Preface - Message to the Reader

What If You Could Help Rebuild the Greatest Library in Human History?

Thousands of years ago, the Library of Alexandria stood as the crown jewel of human achievement — a sanctuary where the collected wisdom of every known civilization was gathered, preserved, and shared freely.

And then, it was lost.

Through fire, conquest, and the slow erosion of time, humanity lost not just books — but ideas, dreams, discoveries, and stories that could have changed the world forever.

Today, the Library of Alexandria lives again — and you are invited to be a part of its restoration.

Our mission is simple yet profound:

To rebuild the greatest library the world has ever known, and to translate all timeless works into every language and dialect, so that no seeker of knowledge is ever left behind again.

By joining our movement to rebuild the modern Library of Alexandria, you become part of an unprecedented mission:

- **Unlimited Access to the Greatest Audiobooks & eBooks Ever Written:**

  Instantly explore thousands of legendary works—Plato, Shakespeare, Jane Austen, Leo Tolstoy, and countless more. All instantly available to read or listen, placing a complete literary universe at your fingertips.

- **Beautiful Paperback & Deluxe Editions at Printing Cost**

  Own any title as an elegant paperback, deluxe hardcover, or stunning collectible boxset—offered to you at true printing cost, delivered straight to your door. Build your personal Library of Alexandria, crafted for beauty, built for durability, and worthy of proud display.

- **Fresh Translations for Modern Readers—in Every Language & Dialect**

  Enjoy timeless masterpieces reimagined in clear, contemporary language—no more outdated phrases or obscure references. Alongside the original versions, we're tirelessly translating these classics into every language and dialect imaginable, ensuring accessibility and understanding across cultures and generations.

- **Join a Global Renaissance of Literature & Knowledge**

  You directly support expanding our library, publishing deluxe editions at true cost, translating works into all global languages, and bringing humanity's greatest stories to people everywhere. By joining today, you're not just preserving a legacy of masterpieces; you set in motion a powerful wave of literary accessibility.

Become a Torchbearer of Knowledge.

Join us for free now at **LibraryofAlexandria.com**

Together, we will ensure that the light of human wisdom never fades again.

With gratitude and a shared love of knowledge,
The Modern Library of Alexandria Team

Visit:

www.libraryofalexandria.com

Or scan the code below:

Introduction

Oracles, Alchemy, and the Cosmos:
The Esoteric Geometry of Being

The Complete Hermeticism Philosophy Collection (Vol. 3) assembles three profound works from the Hermetic and esoteric tradition—The Chaldean Oracles by Julian the Theurgist, Coelum Philosophorum by Paracelsus, and The Emerald Tablet of Thoth attributed to Hermes Trismegistus. Each of these texts offers a distinct but overlapping vision of reality that is deeply symbolic, cosmological, and transformative. They converge around a shared thesis: that the cosmos is not inert matter but a hierarchically ordered spiritual system, and that the human being stands as a mediator between heaven and earth.

These texts challenge linear reason and demand contemplative insight. Their symbolic language invites deep meditation rather than discursive explanation, making them both mysterious and endlessly rewarding. From the prophetic fire-speech of the Chaldean Oracles to the pragmatic spiritual science of Paracelsus and the terse universalism of the Emerald Tablet of Thoth, this collection charts a vast metaphysical landscape of oracular fire, astral order, and inner alchemical power.

This introduction will explore the essence of each text, outlining their individual teachings and showing how, together, they form a trinity of oracular mysticism, operative alchemy, and cosmic Hermeticism. This is not merely philosophy—it is metaphysical initiation.

The Chaldean Oracles:
Theurgic Fire and Celestial Hierarchies

The Chaldean Oracles, attributed to Julian the Theurgist (2nd century CE), are a fragmentary yet luminous set of mystical verses central to the Neoplatonic and later Hermetic traditions. Though their exact origin is obscured by history, they emerged in a period of intense synthesis between Greek philosophy, Babylonian astrology, and Egyptian mysticism.

The Oracles were held in high regard by Neoplatonists like Plotinus, Porphyry, Iamblichus, and Proclus, who saw them as divinely inspired revelations that complement and deepen Platonic philosophy. Their tone is fiery, prophetic, and initiatory, offering a vision of a cosmos infused with divine intelligences and structured through sacred order.

Key concepts include:

- The First Father (One Beyond Being): A hidden source from which all emanates.
- Hecate as Mediator: The divine feminine principle who connects the intelligible and material realms.
- The World Soul and the Cosmic Fire: Fire is not merely physical but a living, animating principle.
- Theurgy as Divine Ascent: Through ritual and purification, the soul rises through the celestial spheres toward its source.

The Oracles speak in paradox and poetic riddles. They do not explain—they initiate. They outline a cosmology in which all levels of being are linked through vibration, fire, and sacred function. For the initiate, these verses offer not information but transformation—a call to awaken the divine spark through theurgy and contemplation.

Coelum Philosophorum:
Alchemy, Nature, and the Medicinal Soul

Paracelsus (1493–1541), the Swiss physician, alchemist, and philosopher, was a towering figure of the Renaissance who united Hermeticism, medicine, and natural philosophy into a singular vision of healing and metaphysical science. Coelum Philosophorum, or The Book of the Heavens of the Philosophers, is one of his core texts—a concise but potent treatise on the principles of spiritual alchemy.

For Paracelsus, alchemy was not merely about the transmutation of metals but the purification and transformation of the soul. He saw the universe as composed of three primary substances—Salt, Sulphur, and Mercury—each corresponding to philosophical, bodily, and energetic principles. His focus was not wealth or gold, but health—physical, psychic, and spiritual.

Core insights include:

- Microcosm and Macrocosm: Man is a reflection of the cosmos, and healing involves restoring harmony between the two.
- Spagyrics: The process of separating, purifying, and recombining to reveal the essence—used both in medicine and spiritual development.
- Nature as Book and Teacher: All of creation is a symbolic script through which divine truths can be read.
- Divine Imagination: The practitioner must possess not only knowledge but vision—the ability to perceive inwardly the forces at work in matter and mind.

Paracelsus rejected scholasticism and insisted on experience, intuition, and direct engagement with nature. He called for a reintegration of science and spirit, and he viewed the physician as both healer and priest—a mediator between the elements and the eternal.

Coelum Philosophorum is thus not just an alchemical text—it is a handbook of divine craftsmanship. It instructs the seeker to observe the world as sacred, to purify the self, and to serve the hidden harmony of life with wisdom, humility, and power.

The Emerald Tablet of Thoth: The Core of Cosmic Hermeticism

This version of The Emerald Tablet, attributed to the Atlantean figure of Thoth-Hermes, expands upon the traditional Hermetic axiom— "As above, so below"—with mystical and cosmological detail. While rooted in the same spiritual lineage as the classic Emerald Tablet, this rendering emphasizes the energetic anatomy of the human being, the spiritual role of the planets, and the vibrational nature of manifestation.

In this account, Thoth is not merely a scribe of divine wisdom, but a living archetype of the spiritual initiate—one who masters the inner sciences of sound, vibration, light, and form. The text blends Atlantean mythology, Hermetic cosmology, and esoteric physics, forming a bridge between myth and metaphysics.

Major themes include:

- The Law of Vibration: All matter is energy in motion, and spiritual mastery involves altering vibrational frequency.
- The Human as Temple: The body contains seven centers aligned with planetary energies, and the spine is the sacred pillar of ascension.
- Immortality through Consciousness: Death is overcome not by resisting time, but by awakening to timelessness through spiritual discipline.
- The Role of the Logos: Spoken word and inner sound are instruments of creation, binding spirit and matter together.

This version of The Emerald Tablet functions as both cosmological scripture and spiritual manual. It points beyond duality toward a unified field of being where the adept no longer distinguishes between the divine and the human, the inner and the outer, the science and the sacred.

The Path of the Hermetic Initiate

Together, these three works reveal a layered vision of spiritual reality and human potential:

- The Chaldean Oracles light the vertical path—rising through hierarchies of fire and light.
- Coelum Philosophorum grounds the path in nature— showing how the soul is healed through harmony with the elements.
- The Emerald Tablet of Thoth fuses the above and below— offering a cosmology where vibration, thought, and will govern all.

These texts do not seek to convert or instruct in the conventional sense. They are invitations—keys for those who are ready to open inner doors. Their value is not measured by how much one understands, but by how deeply one transforms. They require not only study, but practice: meditation, imagination, ritual, and reverence.

The Hermetic initiate is not defined by titles or robes, but by humility, clarity, and a ceaseless hunger for truth. To walk this path is to:

- Speak less, but mean more.
- Live simply, but perceive deeply.
- Master the elements, beginning with the self.
- Serve the One by healing the many.

Welcome to The Complete Hermeticism Philosophy Collection (Vol. 3). May these oracular, alchemical, and cosmic teachings ignite your ascent, deepen your insight, and awaken within you the secret fire of the true Philosopher.

The Chaldean Oracles

Zoroaster

Preface

These Oracles are believed to capture many of the key ideas of Chaldean philosophy. They were passed down to us through Greek translations and were highly respected in ancient times, valued by both early Christian leaders and later Platonists. The teachings are attributed to Zoroaster, though which Zoroaster they refer to is unknown, as historians mention up to six different individuals with that name. It is likely that "Zoroaster" was a title for the leader of the Magi, used as a general term. Scholars offer different ideas about the meaning of the name. One of the more interesting interpretations comes from Kircher, who suggests that it could mean "fashioning images of hidden fire" or "the image of secret things," based on a combination of words. Others say the name comes from terms meaning "one who contemplates the stars."

This collection is acknowledged to be fragmented and incomplete, and many of the original meanings have likely been lost or distorted through translation. Where possible, efforts have been made to clarify confusing expressions, either by refining the Greek translation or adding explanatory notes. Some suggest these Oracles were created by the Greeks, but as Stanley points out, Picus de Mirandula claimed to have the original Chaldean text. According to him, the Greek version contained flaws that did not appear in the original, and he stated that he found the manuscript after Mirandula's death. Additionally, some words in the Greek version are not of Greek origin but have Chaldean roots, adapted to the Greek language.

Berosus is believed to have been the first to introduce Chaldean writings on astronomy and philosophy to the Greeks. It is clear that Chaldean traditions had a significant influence on Greek thought. Taylor believed that some of these mystical sayings inspired the philosophical ideas of Plato, and scholars such as Porphyry, Iamblichus, Proclus, Pletho, and Psellus wrote extensive commentaries on them. The fact that such brilliant thinkers held these Oracles in high regard suggests that they deserve our attention.

The name "Oracles" was likely used to emphasize their deep and mysterious nature. The Chaldeans also had an Oracle that they respected as much as the Greeks revered the Oracle at Delphi. Psellus and Pletho both provided detailed commentary on the Chaldean Oracles. Franciscus Patricius later expanded on their work, adding material from other writers, including Proclus, Hermias, Simplicius, Damascius, Synesius, Olympiodorus, Nicephorus, and Arnobius. Patricius compiled around 324 Oracles, organizing them under various topics. His collection, published in Latin in 1593, served as the foundation for later classifications by Taylor and Cory, and their work was used in preparing the current version.

Some of the Oracles collected by Psellus appear to come from an early Chaldean Zoroaster and are marked with the letter "Z," following Taylor's method, with a few exceptions. Another set is attributed to a group of philosophers called Theurgists, who were active during the reign of Marcus Antoninus, as recorded by Proclus. These are marked with the letter "T." Additional Oracles of uncertain origin are labeled "Z or T," while other passages are credited to individual authors where appropriate.

Introduction

Many people, with good reason, believe that these short and mysterious sayings contain a deep system of mystical philosophy. However, truly understanding this philosophy requires a refined ability to perceive non-physical realities. It is said that the Chaldean Magi passed down their secret knowledge through generations, keeping it alive through tradition from father to son. According to Diodorus, "They do not teach these things as the Greeks do. Among the Chaldeans, philosophy is passed down within families, with sons learning from their fathers. These sons are free from other duties, dedicating themselves fully to learning from their parents, trusting what is taught to them more deeply."

The essence of this oral tradition seems to have survived within these Oracles, which should be studied alongside the teachings of the Kabbalah and Egyptian theology. Those familiar with the Kabbalah know that it can be interpreted in extraordinary ways, especially when paired with the Tarot, which reflects the core ideas of Egyptian theology. If commentators in the past had taken this approach, the Chaldean system within the Oracles would not have been misinterpreted to the extent that it has.

The entire structure of the Hebrew Kabbalah is built on the concept of ten divine powers, each emerging successively from an infinite source of light. These ten powers are seen as the key to understanding all things. They are arranged into three sets of triads, with a tenth power bringing them together. These divine forces extend across four worlds, called Atziluth, Briah, Yetzirah, and Assiah, moving from the most subtle to the most physical. This idea is rooted in pantheism, though it also points toward a divine source. At the heart of all things is the absolute Deity, whose thoughts form the universe we experience.

This same structure applies to the Chaldean system. The diagrams included demonstrate how Chaldean philosophy aligns with the Kabbalah. In the Chaldean view, the "First Mind" and the Intelligible Triad—consisting of Father (Pater), Power (Potentia or Mater), and Mind (Mens)—belong to the realm of higher, non-physical light. The "First Mind" symbolizes the original intelligence that exists within the depths of the divine Father. This intelligence reflects into the "Second Mind," representing divine power in the celestial world. This second mind aligns with the next great triad of divine powers, known as both Intelligible and Intellectual. The third triad belongs to the ethereal world, and it consists of intellectual forces working together.

Finally, the fourth world, known as the Elementary World, is shaped by Hypezokos, or the Flower of Fire, which is the force responsible for building the physical world.

Chaldean theology divided the higher realities into three main levels. The first is Eternal, without a beginning or end, called the "Paternal Depth," the heart of the divine presence. The second is a state of being that has a beginning but no end. This is the Creative World, also known as the Empyrean, which is filled with creations, although its source remains beyond them. The third level is the temporary Ethereal World, which had a beginning in time and will eventually end.

These three worlds are connected by seven spheres. One sphere belongs to the Empyrean, or extends from it, three are part of the Ethereal World, and three exist in the Elementary World, with the physical world uniting them all. These spheres should not be confused with the seven material planets, although the planets represent these spheres physically. The spheres themselves are not material in the usual sense but exist in a deeper, metaphysical way. Psellus tried to link these spheres directly with the planets, but Stanley criticized his approach. However, Stanley's own ideas are not entirely consistent, as he suggests that these worlds are non-physical but also claims that a physical world exists in the Empyrean.

Before the Light of the higher realms, there was the "Paternal Depth," the Absolute Deity that holds all things in potential, always present and unchanging. This idea mirrors the concept of Ain Soph Aur in the Kabbalah—three words, each with three letters, representing three sets of divine powers. These powers become manifest and follow the Triadic Law, guided by the Demiurge, the creator of the universe.

The Light of the higher realms was seen as the first expression of the Paternal Depth, an original and universal essence that flows everywhere and is beyond complete human understanding. The Empyrean is a more refined but still creative fire, serving as the source of the Ethereal World. In turn, the Ethereal World acts as the source for the Elementary World. Through these stages, the ideas of the divine mind become real in time and space.

In many ways, the way of thinking in the East today may not be so different from what it was thousands of years ago. Much that seems strange to us in ancient traditions still resonates with many people around the world. Modern thinkers and scientists have expressed ideas that, while not identical, are similar to these ancient Chaldean beliefs. One example is the idea that natural laws are guided by an intelligent and conscious power. From this point of view, it is not a big leap to see forces as living entities, filling the universe with the creations of the imagination. In this way, history repeats itself, and both ancient and modern ideas reflect the same, ever-changing truth.

Without delving too deeply into metaphysics, it is essential to recognize the importance given to the "Paternal Mind." This is the intelligence of the universe, described poetically as "energizing before energy," which establishes the original patterns of everything that will exist. These patterns are then handed over to the divine powers, known as the Rectores Mundorum, to develop and govern. As the saying goes, "Mind is with Him, power with them."

In the Platonic sense, the word "Intelligible" refers to a way of knowing or perceiving that goes beyond intellectual thought—something higher and distinct from ordinary reasoning. The Chaldeans identified three ways of perceiving: through the senses, through intellectual thought, and through the higher, intelligible concepts. Each of these operates separately, through unique forms or channels. However, their exploration of the soul's nature went much deeper. Though the soul is ultimately connected to the divine, it was seen as a complex being when manifested in existence.

The Oracles speak of the "Paths of the Soul," which are like streams of unyielding fire connecting its essential parts and keeping them whole. These paths, along with its "summits," "fountains," and "vessels," mirror the universal principles that guide everything. This idea, shared by many ancient cosmologies, shows how closely Chaldean metaphysics connect the structure of the universe to the nature of human beings.

In each of the Chaldean Divine Worlds, a group of three divine powers operates together, forming a fourth element that completes the group. As the Oracle says, "In every World, a Triad shines, with the Monad as the ruling principle." These Monads are divine representatives that manage the universe. Each of the four worlds—the Empyrean, Ethereal, Elementary, and Material—is governed by a supreme power that remains directly connected to the Father and guided by divine wisdom. This aligns closely with the Kabbalistic idea of the divine name, which is expressed through four letters in various languages.

The Oracle describes this by saying, "There is a Venerable Name that moves through the Worlds in an unending cycle." The Kabbalah explains this further, teaching that each of the four worlds corresponds to one of the four letters in the divine name. Each world also has its own way of writing this name, reflecting how the order of elements—both on a cosmic and personal level—is governed by the continuous motion of this name. The divine name, associated with the elements, is seen as a universal law that guides creation. This creative force is summed up in the figure known as the Demiurge, or Hypezokos, the "Flower of Fire."

Plato's view of the human being offers a similar idea of the soul's structure. He places intellect in the head, the soul with passions like courage in the heart, and another part of the soul, which contains desires and basic urges, near the stomach and spleen. According to the Chaldean doctrine, as recorded by Psellus, humanity is made up of three types of souls:

First, the Intelligible, or divine soul,

Second, the Intellect or rational soul, and

Third, the Irrational, or passional soul.

This last soul, tied to the body, was thought to change and dissolve at death. The divine soul, according to the Oracles, is described as "a bright fire that, through the Father's power, remains immortal and rules over life." Its influence can only be grasped when the soul moves beyond the illusions created by passions and stops reacting to them.

The rational soul, the Chaldeans taught, can either align itself with the divine or fall under the control of the irrational soul. As the Oracles say, "The divine cannot be reached by those who focus only on the body; only those who strip away these attachments can reach the highest truth." The three types of souls each have their own vehicles. The divine soul's vehicle is immortal, the rational soul's can become immortal through its progress, and the irrational soul is connected to what is called "the image," which is the astral form of the physical body.

Physical life works through these three types of activity. When the body dies, each soul follows a different path, depending on how they used their energies in life. The Oracles encourage people to focus on divine things and resist the urges of the irrational soul, warning, "If you do not succeed, your body will be inhabited by the beasts of the earth."

The Chaldeans assigned the astral form of the irrational soul to the Lunar Sphere. This probably referred to more than just the Moon itself; it included the whole region below the Moon, with Earth at its center. At death, the rational soul rises beyond the Moon's influence, but only if its past life allows for this release. Much importance was placed on how life is lived while the soul is in the body, with frequent calls to seek communion with divine powers. Only the highest form of theurgy was believed to offer such a connection.

"Let the depth of your immortal soul lead you," one Oracle says, "but raise your eyes earnestly upward." Taylor explains this with the idea that "the eyes" represent the soul's inner abilities. When these abilities awaken, the soul becomes filled with a higher life and divine light, almost as if it rises beyond itself.

The Chaldean Magi were said to be the first to separate true visions from dreams. They had a deep understanding of both mental and spiritual realities. Their attention to inner images, along with their passionate devotion, made them more than just teachers—they lived out the philosophy they taught. Life on the open plains of Chaldea, under calm nights and starry skies, nurtured this inner development. From a young age, students of the Magi were taught how to break free from worldly limitations and explore the vast inner realms. One Oracle teaches, "The bonds of the soul, which give her breath, are easy to loosen." Other texts speak of the "Melody of the Ether" and the "Lunar clashings," showing how these mystical experiences reflected real inner practices.

The Oracles also describe how divine visions and impressions appear in the Ether. The Chaldeans believed that the ethers of the elements are the subtle forces through which the more familiar elements—Earth, Air, Water, and Fire—work. These subtle ethers represent the underlying principles of dryness and moisture, heat and cold. The signs of the Zodiac were also linked to these ethers, with each element appearing in three forms. This connection influenced how they understood personality and tendencies. For example, when it was said that someone had Aries rising, it meant that fiery ether dominated their nature, making them energetic and active.

The planets, in turn, were thought to influence the ethers, giving them specific vibrations or energies. These planets, positioned in carefully arranged zones, controlled the flow of these subtle forces throughout the universe.

The Chaldeans believed that the planets were connected not only to specific colors and sounds but also to the ethers, with each planetary force having a special link to certain constellations in the Zodiac. Part of their spiritual practice involved forming connections with these celestial beings. In one fragment, it is said: "If you call upon the celestial Lion often, then, when the heavens disappear from your sight, when the stars lose their light, the moon becomes hidden, and the earth vanishes, you will see everything around you take the shape of a Lion." Both the Chaldeans and Egyptians had a deep understanding of color, which reflected their heightened spiritual awareness. Bright colors were thought to awaken the mind's ability to imagine and engage with inner visions.

The Chaldean method of contemplation involved becoming one with the object of meditation, similar to the process used in Indian Yoga. This approach is captured in the saying, "He becomes one with the images, casting them around himself." Though the divine is without form or body, it was believed that divine forces become temporarily bound to forms for the benefit of humanity.

The subtle ethers served as coverings for the divine Light. The Oracles teach that beyond these ethers lies "a solar world and endless Light." This divine Light was the object of their deepest reverence. However, the Light they sought was not the light of the sun we know. Instead, it was referred to as "the starless sphere above," where "the more true Sun" resides. Theosophists understand this as the idea that the physical sun is just a reflection of a higher, more glorious light.

Some individuals, through their strength, could reach this Light on their own. As the Oracles say, "The mortal who approaches the fire will receive Light from the divine, and the immortal ones are swift to aid those who persevere." However, even those less capable were not entirely left out. The Oracles explain, "Some are blessed with knowledge even as they sleep, drawing strength from the divine." This idea inspired many later thinkers, including Porphyry and Synesius. Apuleius's Metamorphoses and the Vision of Scipio also reflect this belief. Though many Christians are familiar with the saying "He gives to His beloved in sleep," few fully grasp the deeper meaning behind it.

What, then, was the Chaldean view of earthly life? Were they pessimistic, dismissing the material world as unimportant? It seems more accurate to say that their philosophy was filled with spiritual hope. They believed that beyond the limits of matter lay a better and truer reality. Earthly life was seen as a flawed reflection of this higher realm. Like us, the Chaldeans sought what is good, beautiful, and true.

But unlike those who chase external pleasures, they understood that true fulfillment is found within.

The first step in this journey toward inner fulfillment was living a simple life. For most of the Magi, this way of life was ingrained from birth. The discipline of living simply, combined with wisdom, made them especially open to nature's truths. As one Oracle warns: "Do not descend into the dark, glittering world below. Beneath the earth lies a steep fall, where a throne of destructive power awaits. Do not go down into that deceptive splendor, for it will only defile your inner light. Its brilliance is false, and it is home only to the children of sorrow." This beautifully expresses the idea that pursuing physical pleasures diminishes the soul's higher energy. Yet, for those who live virtuously and purify themselves, the Oracles offer encouragement: "The higher powers build up the bodies of the holy ones."

The law of karma was just as important in Chaldean thought as it is in modern theosophy. Ficinus explains, "The soul moves continuously, passing through everything in its journey. Once this journey is complete, it must return through the same paths, weaving a new cycle of life, as Zoroaster teaches: whenever the same causes arise, the same effects will follow."

This is the deeper meaning behind the saying "History repeats itself," far removed from superstitious ideas of fate. Here, everyone receives what they deserve based on their actions, whether good or bad. These are the bonds of life. Yet, the Oracles warn, "Do not expand your destiny," urging people to explore the "River of the Soul." Though the soul serves the body, it can still rise back to the divine order from which it came by combining sacred actions with reason.

We are encouraged to understand the Intelligible, that divine part of being which lies beyond the mind. This can only be grasped with the highest potential of our intellect. The Oracles say, "Understand the Intelligible with the bright flame of an awakened mind." Zoroaster is also credited with saying, "The one who knows himself knows everything within himself." Another teaching suggests that "The

Paternal Mind has planted symbols within the soul." However, such knowledge was only available to Theurgists, who, as the Oracles explain, "do not fall into the same fate as the masses." The divine light cannot shine in a disordered soul, just as clouds block the sun. Those who seek higher wisdom without preparation or purity walk a path filled with confusion and darkness, and their efforts will fail.

Even though our destiny may be "written in the stars," the divine soul's mission is to raise the human soul above the circle of necessity. The Oracles praise the power of a will that triumphs over obstacles, describing it like this:

"Hewing down walls with the force of magic, Breaking apart the barriers, Splitting the seven posts to pieces, Speaking the words of mastery!"

This triumph comes through strengthening the will and elevating the imagination, which has the power to guide consciousness. As the Oracles say, "Believe yourself to be beyond the body, and you will be." They might have added, "Then your purified imagination will reveal the symbols of the soul." Yet, when looking within, one must confront the self honestly. "On beholding yourself, fear," meaning you must face the imperfect parts of yourself.

To achieve the highest perfection, everything must be viewed as ideal. Willpower is the key to mystical progress, having a powerful influence over the body's nervous system. Through will, fleeting visions can be held steady within the astral light. Will also drives consciousness toward communion with the divine. However, the challenge lies in aligning three distinct wills—the wills of the Divine Soul, the Rational Soul, and the Irrational Soul.

Selfishness blocks the flow of higher thought, keeping it tied to the body. This is not just a moral idea but a scientific truth. Selfishness beyond basic needs is nothing more than vulgarity. Just as a picture that seems beautiful to a refined mind might look like a mess of colors to someone untrained, so too the broad perspective of one who sees beyond personal concerns cannot be understood by those focused only on themselves.

The path to the greatest good lies through self-sacrifice—offering up the lower self to serve the higher self. Behind this higher self is the hidden presence of the "Ancient of Days," the unified essence of divine humanity. These truths are grasped only by the soul. The soul's song can only be heard in the sacred silence where the divine dwells.

The Oracles of Zoroaster

CAUSE. GOD.

FATHER	MIND	FIRE
MONAD	DYAD	TRIAD.

God is described as having the head of a hawk. He is the first and eternal being, beyond corruption, not created by anything else, whole and unchanging, unlike anything else. He gives all good things, cannot be destroyed, and is the highest good and the wisest. He is the source of fairness, justice, and wisdom, teaching Himself and embodying perfection. He is the inspiration for Sacred Philosophy. Eusebius, Præparatio Evangelica, Book 1, Chapter 10. This Oracle isn't found in ancient collections or in the writings of medieval occultists. Cory seems to have found it in Eusebius's writings, where the Persian Zoroaster is credited as its author.

Theurgists say that this God is both old and young. They describe Him as a God who moves endlessly, whose power fills the universe, and who controls everything that moves. He has limitless energy and exerts a force that spirals throughout creation. Proclus on Plato's Timaeus, 244. Z. or T. p. 24 In Egyptian mythology, there were two Horuses—an older and younger God—both sons of Osiris and Isis. Taylor suggests that this passage refers to Kronos, or Time, called Chronos by later Platonists. In Roman mythology, Kronos (also called Saturnus) was the son of Uranus and Gaia, married to Rhea, and father of Zeus.

The God of the Universe is eternal and boundless, both young and old, with a spiraling force. Cory includes this Oracle in his collection but doesn't mention its source. Lobeck questioned its authenticity.

The Eternal Æon, according to the Oracle, is the reason for endless life, boundless strength, and tireless energy. Taylor.—T.

The divine ones call this unknowable God "silent" and say He communicates through the power of the Mind. Human souls can only understand Him using their minds. Proclus in Theology of Plato, 321. T. The word "inscrutable" is used, though Taylor translates it as "stable," and some suggest "incomprehensible" might be a better term.

The Chaldeans call this God Dionysos (or Bacchus) and Iao in the Phoenician language, referring to Him as the "Intelligible Light." He is also called Sabaoth, meaning He is above the Seven Spheres and acts as the Demiurge. Lydus, De Mensibus, 83. T.

He holds all things within Himself, at the peak of His existence, yet He also exists beyond everything. Proclus in Theology of Plato, 212. T. "Hyparxis" usually refers to "existence" or "subsistence." "Hupar" suggests reality as distinct from appearance, and "Huparche" means "beginning."

He measures and defines all things. Proclus in Theology of Plato, 386. T. The phrase "Thus he speaks the words" appears in the Greek text but is omitted by Taylor and Cory.

Nothing imperfect comes from the Paternal Principle. Psellus, 38; Pletho. Z. This suggests that imperfection only appears through later processes of creation.

The Father did not bring forth fear; instead, He gave the gift of persuasion. Pletho. Z.

The Father fully understands Himself and doesn't limit His fire to His intellectual power alone. Psellus, 30; Pletho, 33. Z. p. 26 Taylor interprets this as "The Father withdrew Himself quickly but didn't confine His fire to His mind." However, the Greek text doesn't mention "quickly." The word "Arpazo" can mean "grasp" or "understand with the mind."

This is the kind of Mind that exists before action begins, staying in the Father's depth and nourishing silence in the hidden place of God. Proclus on Timaeus, 167. T.

Everything comes from the same divine fire. The Father created everything perfectly and passed it to the Second Mind, whom all nations refer to as the First. Psellus, 24; Pletho, 30. Z.

The Second Mind governs the Empyrean World. Damascius, On Principles. T.

The Intelligible speaks by understanding. Psellus, 35. Z.

- Power belongs to them, but the source of Mind is from Him. Proclus in Plato's Theology, 365. T.
- The Father's Mind rides upon delicate Guides, which shine with the trails of unwavering and unstoppable Fire. Proclus on Plato's Cratylus. T.
- …After the Father's thought, I, the Soul, take my place, a warmth that gives life to all things. …For He placed The Intelligible within the Soul, and the Soul within the lifeless body, Just as the Father of Gods and Men has placed these within us. Proclus in Timaeus, 124. Z. or T.
- Nature's works exist together with the Father's light of understanding. The Soul decorated the vast Heaven, and after the Father, it continues to shape it. But her rule remains high above. Proclus in Timaeus, 106. Z. or T. The word "dominion" is from the Greek krata, though some versions use kcrata, meaning "horns."
- The Soul, as a shining Fire through the Father's power, remains immortal, ruling over Life and filling the deep places of the World's heart. Psellus, 28; Pletho, 11. Z.
- With the channels intertwined, the Soul carries out the works of eternal Fire. Proclus in Politico, p. 399. Z. or T.

- The Fire from beyond does not lock its power in matter but exists within the Mind. For it is the Mind of Mind that shapes the Fiery World. Proclus in Theology, 333, and Timaeus, 157. T.

- The one who first came from Mind wraps one Fire within another, weaving them together to unite the flowing fountains of Fire while keeping its brilliance untouched. Proclus in Parmenides. T.

- A Fiery Whirlwind draws down the glow of flashing flames, penetrating the Universe's depths, as its marvelous rays extend downwards from there. Proclus in Plato's Theology, 171 and 172. T.

- The Monad came first into existence and still remains as the Paternal Monad. Proclus in Euclid, 27. T.

- When the Monad stretches outward, the Dyad is born. Proclus in Euclid, 27. T. The Pythagoreans describe the Monad, Dyad, and Triad just as Plato does with Bound, Infinite, and Mixed. These Oracles use the terms Hyparxis, Power, and Energy for the same ideas. Damascius On Principles. Taylor.

- Beside Him sits the Dyad, sparkling with intellectual divisions. It governs all things and brings order to whatever lacks it. Proclus in Plato's Theology, 376. T.

- The Father's Mind declared that all things should be divided into Three, and with His Will's agreement, everything was immediately separated this way. Proclus in Parmenides. T.

- The Eternal Father's Mind spoke of the Three, ruling everything through understanding. Proclus in Timaeus. T.

- The Father blended every Spirit from within this Triad. Lydus, De Mensibus, 20. Taylor.

- Everything flows from the heart of this Triad. Lydus, De Mensibus, 20. Taylor.

- Everything is ruled by and exists within this Triad. Proclus in First Alcibiades. T.

You must understand that everything bows before the Three Supreme Powers. Damascius, On Principles. T.

From this source comes the Form of the Triad, which existed before creation. It is not the first Essence but the principle by which all things are measured. Anon. Z. or T.

In it appeared Virtue, Wisdom, and all-knowing Truth. Anon. Z. or T.

In every World, the Triad shines brightly, and above it all, the Monad reigns supreme. Damascius in Parmenides. T.

The first course is Sacred. In the middle course, the Sun moves, and in the third, the Earth is warmed by inner fire. Anon. Z. or T.

It stands high above, giving life to Light, Fire, Ether, and Worlds. Simplicius in his Physics, 143. Z. or T.

Ideas

INTELLIGIBLES, INTELLECTUALS, IYNGES, SYNOCHES, TELETARCHÆ, FOUNTAINS, PRINCIPLES, HECATE AND DÆMONS.

1. The Mind of the Father spun forth with a roaring sound, grasping with unshakable Will every possible Idea. These Ideas, which flowed from a single source, were released, for both the Will and the Purpose came from the Father, and through changing forms of life, they remain connected to Him. But these Ideas were separated and spread by Intellectual Fire into other forms of Intelligence. Before the diverse World took shape, the King of All placed an intellectual and unchanging Pattern as a model. The impression of this Pattern spread throughout the World, filling the Universe with many kinds of Ideas, yet all these Ideas share a single origin. From this one foundation, they split and spread across different bodies throughout the Universe, moving endlessly through

the depths, shining and radiating outward without end. These are intellectual concepts from the Father's Fountain, filled with the brightness of Fire, carried by the flow of unceasing Time. The Father's original, perfect Fountain released these first-born Ideas. Proclus in Parmenidem. Z. or T.

2. These Ideas, though many, flash down onto the shining Worlds, carrying with them the Three Divine Powers. Damascius in Parmenidem. T.

3. They guard the works of the Father and the One Mind, which holds all understanding. Proclus in Theologiam Platonis, 205. T.

4. All things exist together within the World of Pure Intelligence. Damascius, De Principiis. T.

5. Every form of Intelligence knows the Divine, for Intelligence cannot exist without the object of its understanding, and the object of understanding cannot exist apart from Intelligence. Damascius. Z. or T.

6. Intelligence depends on what it understands, and without this connection, it cannot exist. Proclus, Th. Pl., 172. Z. or T.

7. Through Intelligence, He holds together the things that can be understood and brings the Soul into the Worlds.

8. With Intelligence, He gathers what can be known and brings Sensation into the Worlds. Proclus in Crat. T.

9. The Father's Intelligence, which knows all things and beautifies what cannot be expressed, has scattered symbols throughout the World. Proclus in Cratylum. T.

10. This structure is the starting point of all division. Damascius, De Principiis. T.

11. Pure Understanding is the root of every division. Damascius, De Principiis. T.

12. Pure Understanding serves as nourishment for what gains knowledge. Damascius, De Principiis. T.

13. The oracles describe the Order as existing before the Heavens, beyond words, and say it possesses Mystic Silence. Proclus in Cratylum. T.

14. The oracle explains that causes born from Understanding are swift. It says that after flowing from the Father, they quickly return to Him again. Proclus in Cratylum. T.

15. These Natures are both Intelligent and objects of Intelligence. They hold knowledge within themselves and become subjects for others to understand. Proclus, Theologiam Platonis. T.

The Second Order of Platonic philosophy is called the "Intelligible and Intellectual Triad." In Chaldean teachings, this order includes the Iynges, Synoches, and Teletarchs. The later Platonists' Intellectual Triad corresponds with the Chaldean Fountains, Fontal Fathers, or Cosmagogi.

16. The Iynges gain their understanding from the Father. Through mysterious guidance, they are moved to comprehend. Psellus, 41; Pletho, 31. Z.

17. It is the Operator and the Giver of Life-bearing Fire. It fills Hecate's life-giving womb and transfers the empowering energy of Fire to the Synoches, endowing them with immense strength. Proclus in Timaeus, 128. T.

18. He gave His Whirlwinds to guard the Supernals, blending His own force within the Synoches. Dam., On Principles. T.

19. Likewise, many others serve the material Synoches. T.

20. The Teletarchs are part of the Synoches. Dam., On Principles. T.

21. Rhea, the source and river of blessed intellects, holds the powers of all things in her sacred womb, pouring out continuous creation upon everything. Proclus in Cratylus. T.

22. She marks the boundary of the Father's Depth and serves as the source of intellect. Dam., On Principles. T.

23. He shines with clear, radiant strength, filled with intellectual energy. Dam. T.

24. His brilliance contains intellectual power, spreading love throughout everything. Dam. T.

25. All things submit to the swirling motions of the Intellectual Fire, following the Father's wise guidance. Proclus in

Parmenides. T.

26. Oh, how the World is governed by unyielding Intellectual Rulers.

27. Hecate's source aligns with that of the Fontal Fathers. T.

28. From Him leap forth the Amilicti, unrelenting thunderbolts, and the whirlwinds that fill Hecate's sacred womb with unstoppable strength. He surrounds the brilliance of Fire, and His mighty Spirit, burning beyond, rules the Poles. Proclus in Cratylus. T.

29. There is another source that leads the Empyrean World. Proclus in Timaeus. Z. or T.

30. It is the source of all sources and the boundary of every spring. Dam., On Principles.

31. The fountain that generates life for Souls is contained within two Minds. Dam., On Principles. T.

32. Beneath these exists the Primary One of all non-material things. Dam. in Parmenides. Z. or T.

Following the Intellectual Triad is the Demiurgos, from whom came the Essences and Orders, including various spirits and the material world.

33. Light born from the Father alone holds the power to grasp His Mind. It pours understanding into all sources and principles, driving their endless cycles. Proclus in Timaeus, 242.

34. All sources and principles revolve continuously, never ceasing their motion. Proclus in Parmenides. Z. or T.

35. The principles that have understood the Father's plans are wrapped in physical forms and bodies. These serve as links between the Father and matter, making invisible ideas visible in the world. Dam., On Principles. Z. or T.

36. Typhon, Echidna, and Python, children of Tartarus and Gaia, joined by Uranus, form a Chaldean Triad that watches over and controls chaotic creations. Olymp. in Phaedrus. T.

37. Some irrational demons, without thought, are sustained by the

rulers of the air. This is why the oracle says, "They guide the airy, earthly, and water-dwelling creatures." Olymp. in Phaedrus. T.

38. When connected to divine beings, the word "Aquatic" signifies rule tied to water. This is why the oracle calls the aquatic gods "Water Walkers." Proclus in Timaeus, 270. T.

39. Some water spirits, known as Nereids in Orpheus's writings, dwell in high, misty waters, appearing in the damp air. As Zoroaster taught, these spirits can sometimes be seen by those with keen sight, especially in Persia and Africa. Ficino, On the Immortality of the Soul, 123. T.

Particular Souls

SOUL, LIFE, MAN.

1. The Father created ideas, and He gave life to all mortal bodies. Proclus in Tim., 336. T.

2. The Father of gods and humans placed the Mind (nous) in the Soul (psyche) and placed both within the human body.

3. The Father's Mind planted symbols within the Soul. Psellus, 26; Pletho, 6. Z.

4. He mixed the Vital Spark from two substances—Mind and Divine Spirit—and as a third element, He added Holy Love, the sacred Charioteer that unites all things. Lydus, De Mensibus, 3.

5. This Love fills the Soul with deep affection. Proclus in Platonis Theologia, 4. Z. or T.

6. The human Soul embraces God closely. It holds no mortal nature and is entirely filled with God's presence, rejoicing in the harmony that sustains the mortal body. Psellus, 17; Pletho, 10. Z.

7. Stronger Souls can see Truth by their own nature and are more creative. According to the Oracle, such Souls are saved by their own power. Proclus in I. Alcibiades. Z.

8. The Oracle says that ascending Souls sing hymns of praise. Olympiodorus in Phaedrus. Z. or T.

9. Of all Souls, the most blessed are those sent from Heaven to Earth. They are joyful and possess indescribable strength, for they come from your radiant essence, O King, or from Jove himself, driven by the unbreakable power of Mithus. Synesius, De Insomniis, 153. Z. or T.

10. The Souls of those who die suddenly are the purest. Psellus, 27. Z.

11. The threads that hold the Soul's breath can be easily released. Psellus, 32; Pletho, 8. Z.

12. When one Soul is set free, the Father sends another to keep the number complete. Z. or T.

13. By understanding the Father's works, these Souls escape the grasp of Fate. They remain in God's presence, drawing strong lights that descend from the Father. As they descend, the Soul gathers the heavenly fruit, the flower that nourishes the spirit. Proclus in Tim., 321. Z. or T.

14. This spiritual force, which the blessed call the Pneumatic Soul, becomes a god, a powerful spirit, or an image without a body. In this form, the Soul experiences punishment. The Oracles say that the Soul's tasks in Hades resemble the deceptive visions of a dream. Synesius, De Insomniis. Z. or T. The term "Dæmon" originally referred to both good and bad spirits, often applied to pure beings as much as to impure ones. This concept aligns with the Eastern teaching of Devachan, a state of pleasant illusion after death.

15. Life flows from many sources, moving from above, through the opposite side, to the center of the Earth. From there, it reaches the fiery middle point, where the life-giving fire descends into the physical world. Z. or T.

16. Water represents life, which is why Plato and the ancient gods described the Soul as both the water that gives life and the fountain from which it flows. Proclus in Tim., 318. Z.

17. O Man, daring by nature, you are a subtle creation. Psellus, 12;

Pletho, 21. Z.

18. Your body will become the home of the beasts of the Earth. Psellus, 36; Pletho, 7. Z. The body is the vessel that temporarily holds the Mind (nous).

19. The Soul moves continuously through different experiences over time. Once these experiences are complete, it must pass through everything again, weaving the same pattern of life in the world. Zoroaster believed that when the same causes arise, the same effects will inevitably follow. Ficinus, De Immortalitate Animæ, 129. Z.

20. According to Zoroaster, the Soul's ethereal form continually returns through reincarnation. Ficinus, De Immortalitate Animæ, 131. Z.

21. The Oracles celebrate the essential source of every Soul, which flows from the Empyrean, the Ethereal, and the Material realms. They separate this source from Zoogonothea, the life-giving goddess Rhea. From her, they create two orders: one related to the Soul and the other to Fate. The Oracles teach that the Soul comes from the animating order but sometimes falls under the control of Fate. When this happens, the Soul enters an irrational state and becomes subject to Fate instead of Divine Providence. Proclus, De Providentia apud Fabricium, Bibliotheca Graeca, vol. 8, 486. Z. or T.

Matter

THE WORLD--AND NATURE.

1. The Matrix contains everything within it. T.
2. It can be divided entirely, yet it also remains whole.
3. From it flows the endless creation of many different types of Matter. Proclus in *Tim.*, 118. T.
4. These creations form atoms, physical shapes, material bodies, and everything that belongs to the realm of matter. Damascius, *De Principiis*. T.

5. The Nymphs of the Fountains, along with all Water Spirits and forms of the Earth, sky, and stars, are the Riders and Rulers of Matter—whether celestial, starry, or deep within the Abyss. Lydus, p. 32.

6. The Oracles teach that Evil is weaker than even nothingness. Proclus, *De Providentia*. Z. or T.

7. Matter fills the whole world, as the gods also proclaim. Proclus, *Tim.*, 142. Z. or T.

8. Although Divine Beings have no bodies, they are bound to bodies for our sake. Since bodies cannot fully hold spiritual beings due to the limits of material nature, this connection exists to focus the divine within us. Proclus in *Platonis Politicus*, 359. Z. or T.

9. The Father's Mind, understanding His creations, spread the fiery bonds of love throughout everything, ensuring that all things would remain connected in love for eternity. This way, everything in creation stays linked to the Father's Light, and the elements of the world are drawn together by mutual attraction. Proclus in *Tim.*, 155. T.

10. The Maker of everything, acting through His own power, shaped the World. Out of a fiery mass, He formed all things by His will, making the Universe a visible creation, not hidden or shapeless. Proclus in *Tim.*, 154. Z. or T.

11. He made all things in His own likeness, casting them in the image of His form.

12. They reflect His Mind, but because they are made, they also contain something physical. Proclus in *Tim.*, 87. Z. or T.

13. There is a Holy Name that moves without rest, leaping into the worlds through the Father's rapid vibrations. Proclus in *Cratylus*. Z. or T.

14. The ethers of the elements are present there. Olympiodorus in *Phaedrus*. Z. or T.

15. The Oracles reveal that divine symbols and other visions appear within the Ether or Astral Light. Simplicius in *Physica*, 144. Z. or T.

16. In this realm, the shapeless takes form. Simplicius in *Physica*, 143. Z. or T.

17. These are the hidden and revealed impressions of the World.

18. The World that resists the Light draws many down through twisting currents. Proclus in *Tim.*, 339. Z. or T.

19. He made the whole world from Fire, Air, Water, Earth, and nourishing Ether. Z. or T.

20. He placed the Earth in the center, Water beneath it, and Air above both. Z. or T.

21. He fixed countless stars in place, keeping them steady and unmoving, with no labor but by stable order, forcing Fire into Fire. Proclus in *Tim.*, 280. Z. or T.

22. The Father gathered the seven layers of the Cosmos, shaping the Heavens in a curved form. Damascius in *Parmenides*. Z. or T.

23. He created the seven wandering bodies (the planets). Z. or T.

24. Their movements were set within well-organized zones. Z. or T.

25. He made six of them, placing the Fiery Sun as the seventh in the center. Proclus in *Tim.*, 280. Z. or T.

26. From the center, all lines extend equally in every direction. Proclus in *Euclidem.*

27. The Sun moves continuously around this central point. Proclus in *Platonis Theologia*, 317. Z. or T.

28. It eagerly races toward the center of brilliant Light. Proclus in *Tim.*, 236. T.

29. The Great Sun and the Shining Moon.

30. Its rays spread outward like flowing hair, ending in sharp points. Proclus in *Platonis Politicus*, 387. T.

31. The movements of the Sun and Moon, the silent spaces of the sky, and the music of Ether join together with the phases of the Sun, Moon, and Air. Proclus in *Tim.*, 257. Z. or T.

32. The most mysterious teachings say that His completeness is found in the realms beyond this world, where a Solar World and endless Light exist, as the Chaldean Oracles proclaim.

Proclus in *Tim.*, 264. Z. or T.

33. The Sun is the truest measure of time, for it is itself the time of all time, as the Oracle of the gods teaches. Proclus in *Tim.*, 249. Z. or T.

34. The Sun's disk moves through the starless region above the unchanging sphere and is not among the planets but within the three worlds, according to mystical teachings. Julian, *Cratylus*, 5, 334. Z. or T.

35. The Sun is Fire, a channel of Fire, and a distributor of Fire. Proclus in *Tim.*, 141. Z. or T.

36. Thus, Kronos, through the Sun, observes the true pole.

37. The movements of Ether, the Moon's great path, and the changing flows of Air. Proclus in *Tim.*, 257. Z. or T.

38. O Ether, Sun, and Spirit of the Moon, you are the rulers of the Air. Proclus in *Tim.*, 257. Z. or T.

39. The wide sky, the Moon's path, and the Sun's pole. Proclus in *Tim.*, 257. Z. or T.

40. The Goddess brings forth the mighty Sun and the bright Moon.

41. She gathers their light, absorbing the music of Ether, the Sun, the Moon, and all that exists in the Air.

42. Tireless Nature governs the worlds and their motions, ensuring that the Heavens move in an eternal cycle, so the rhythms of the Sun, Moon, seasons, day, and night are fulfilled. Proclus in *Tim.*, 4, 323. Z. or T.

43. And above the shoulders of the Great Goddess, vast Nature is exalted. Proclus in *Tim.*, 4. T.

44. The greatest thinkers of Babylon, along with Ostanes and Zoroaster, rightly call the starry spheres "Herds"—either because they alone move perfectly around a center or because, as the Oracles suggest, they gather the principles of nature, which are also called "Herds" (agelous). Adding a "gamma" makes them "Angels" (aggelous). This is why the stars that govern these herds are viewed as divine beings or spirits like Angels and are called Archangels, numbering seven.

Anonymous in *Theologumenis Arithmeticis*. Z.

45. Zoroaster describes the alignment between physical forms and the Soul's ideals as "Divine Allurements." Ficinus, *De Vita Cælitus Comparanda*. Z.

Magical And Philosophical Precepts

1. Do not focus your mind on the vast lands of the Earth, for the Plant of Truth does not grow from the ground. Do not try to measure the Sun's movements by creating rules, for it moves by the Father's Eternal Will, not just for your benefit. Let go of the Moon's restless path, for it always moves by the force of necessity. The Stars were not created just for you. The flight of birds through the sky reveals no truth, nor does the examination of animal sacrifices—these are mere illusions, tricks used for profit. Stay away from these if you wish to enter the sacred paradise of devotion, where Virtue, Wisdom, and Justice meet. Psellus, 4. Z.

2. Do not lower yourself to the shadowy, splendid World, where there lies a deceptive Depth and Hades, wrapped in clouds, filled with unintelligible images. This dark abyss is treacherous and endlessly churning, always joined with a lifeless and formless body. Synesius, *De Insomniis*, 140. Z. or T.

3. Do not descend, for beneath the Earth lies a cliff, reached by a ladder with seven steps, and on that path rests the Throne of a destructive and fateful force. Psellus, 6; Pletho, 2. Z.

4. Do not linger at the edge of the cliff, trapped in material filth, for your true form belongs to a radiant realm. Psellus, 1, 2; Pletho, 14; Synesius, 140. Z.

5. Do not call upon the visible form of Nature's Soul. Psellus, 15; Pletho, 23. Z.

6. Do not seek Nature, for her name brings ruin. Proclus in *Platonis Theologia*, 143. Z.

7. You should not look upon them before your body is initiated, for their allure draws souls away from the sacred mysteries.

Proclus in *I. Alcibiades*. Z. or T.

8. Do not bring her forth, or she may take something with her when she leaves. Psellus, 3; Pletho, 15. Z. (Taylor says that "her" refers to the human soul.)

9. Do not corrupt the Spirit or delve too deeply into superficial matters. Psellus, 19; Pletho, 13. Z.

10. Do not seek to expand your destiny. Psellus, 37; Pletho, 4.

11. The Oracle says not to step beyond what is required for devotion. Damascius, *Vita Isidori*. Z. or T.

12. Do not change the sacred names used in invocations, for in every language, God has provided sacred names with great power. Psellus, 7; Nicephorus. Z. or T.

13. Do not go out when the official passes by. Picus de Mirandola, *Conclusions*. Z.

14. Let fiery hope sustain you on the angelic plane. Olympiodorus in *Phaedrus*; Proclus in *Alcibiades*. Z. or T.

15. The glowing Fire comes first, and those who approach it will receive Light from God. The blessed Immortals respond swiftly to those who persevere. Proclus in *Tim.*, 65. Z. or T.

16. The gods urge us to understand the radiating form of Light. Proclus in *Cratylus*. Z. or T.

17. You must hasten toward the Light and the Rays of the Father, who sent you a Soul (Psyche) endowed with deep Mind (Nous). Psellus, 33; Pletho, 6. Z.

18. Seek the path to Paradise. Psellus, 41; Pletho, 27. Z.

19. Learn what is beyond Mind, for it exists beyond understanding. Psellus, 41; Pletho, 27. Z.

20. There is one Intelligible Being whom you must grasp with the finest part of your Mind. Psellus, 31; Pletho, 28. Z.

21. The Paternal Mind will not accept the soul's longing until it awakens from forgetfulness and remembers the sacred symbol of the Father. Psellus, 39; Pletho, 5. Z.

22. Some are given the ability to know the Light, while others, even in sleep, are blessed with insight from the Father's strength. Synesius, *De Insomniis*, 135. Z. or T.

23. You must approach the Intelligible Being not with force but with a calm, searching mind, measuring all things except this Being. If you incline your Mind gently, you will understand it—not with effort, but with a pure, inquisitive sense. Stretch your Soul toward this higher understanding, for it lies beyond ordinary thought. Damascius. T.

24. You cannot grasp it in the same way you understand common things. Damascius, *De Primis Principiis*. T.

25. Those who understand must know the deep mysteries of the Paternal Mind beyond this world. Damascius. Z. or T.

26. Divine truths are not accessible to those focused only on the body. They can only be known by those who, stripped of their earthly attachments, reach the highest summit. Proclus in *Cratylus*. Z. or T.

27. Clothed in the strength of radiant Light, with triple power protecting both Soul and Mind, one must fill the Mind with sacred symbols and focus, not wander along the celestial path without direction.

28. Armed with every kind of strength, he becomes like the Goddess. Proclus in *Platonis Theologia*, 324. T.

29. Explore the River of the Soul—know where you came from and in what order. Even though you have served the body, rise again to the place from which you descended by aligning your actions with sacred reason. Psellus, 5; Pletho, 1. Z.

30. Fiery rays extend in all directions toward the freed Soul. Psellus, 11; Pletho, 24. Z.

31. Let the infinite depth of your Soul guide you, and raise your eyes upward with purpose. Psellus, 11; Pletho, 20.

32. As a rational being, you must control your Soul so it avoids earthly misfortune and finds salvation. Lydus, *De Mensibus*, 2.

33. If you direct your fiery Mind toward devotion, you will preserve the fragile body. Psellus, 22; Pletho, 16. Z.

34. A life purified by Divine Fire removes every stain and all irrational impulses that cling to the Soul during its earthly

existence, as the Oracle teaches us to believe. Proclus in *Tim.*, 331. Taylor.

35. The Oracles state that purification rituals benefit not only the Soul but also the body, making it fit to receive help and health. These teachings are given by the gods to the most devoted Theurgists. Julian, *Cratylus*, 334. Z. or T.

36. The Oracle warns us to avoid following the masses blindly. Proclus in *I. Alcibiades*. Z. or T.

37. He who knows himself knows everything within himself. Picus, p. 211. Z.

38. The Oracles emphasize that we have the power to choose, rather than being ruled by the natural order. For example, they say, "When you look at yourself, be mindful," and "If you believe you are more than your body, then you are." Furthermore, they teach that "Our personal struggles shape the kind of life we create." Proclus, *De Providentia*, p. 483. Z. or T.

39. These are deep mysteries I explore in the profound Abyss of the Mind.

40. The Oracle says that God does not abandon us unless we approach divine matters with confusion or impurity. If we do so, our progress is incomplete, our efforts are wasted, and the path becomes dark. Proclus in *Parmenides*. Z. or T.

41. If you do not recognize that every god is good, you remain vigilant for nothing. Proclus in *Platonis Politicus*, 355. Z. or T.

42. Theurgists do not fall into the ranks of those controlled by Fate. Lydus, *De Mensibus*. Taylor.

43. The number nine, composed of three triads, reaches the highest level of theology, as the Chaldean philosophy teaches through Porphyry. Lydus, p. 121.

44. On Hecate's left side is a fountain of Virtue that remains untouched and pure. Psellus, 13; Pletho, 9. Z.

45. Even the Earth mourned for them and their children. Psellus, 21; Pletho, 3. Z.

46. The Furies are the enforcers of punishment upon humans. Psellus, 26; Pletho, 19. Z.

47. Do not become trapped by the Furies of Earth or the demands of nature, or you will perish. Proclus in *Theologia*, 297. Z. or T.

48. Nature teaches us that there are pure spirits, and that even the harmful seeds of matter can be transformed into something useful and good. Psell., 16; Pletho, 18. Z.

49. You only need to offer sacrifices for three days, no more. Pic. Concl. Z.

50. Before anything else, the priest in charge of the works of fire must sprinkle water from the roaring sea. Proc. in Crat. Z. or T.

51. Work diligently around the sacred wheel of Hecate. Psell., 9. Nicephorus.

52. When you see an earthly spirit approaching, shout out loud and offer the stone Mnizourin as a sacrifice. Psell., 40. Z.

53. If you call upon these forces often, you will notice everything around you fading into darkness. The sky will no longer be visible, the stars will lose their light, and the moon will be hidden. The Earth itself will feel absent, lightning will flash around you, and thunder will fill the air. Psell., 10; Pletho, 22. Z.

54. From the depths of the Earth will spring forth demons with the faces of dogs, offering no real sign to guide mortals. Psell., 23; Pletho, 10. Z.

55. A similar fire will rush through the air, formless and chaotic, bringing with it the sound of a voice or a swirling flash of light. You may see the vision of a fiery horse, or a child riding on a celestial steed—either clothed in gold, naked, or shooting arrows of light while standing on the horse's shoulders. If you focus deeply in meditation, you will be able to unite these visions into the image of a lion. Proc. in Pl. Polit., 380; Stanley Hist. Philos. Z. or T.

56. When you see the holy, formless fire shining through the

depths of the universe, listen closely and hear the voice of the fire. Psell., 14; Pletho, 25. Z.

Oracles From Porphyry

1. Above the celestial lights, there is an eternal flame that sparkles without end. It is the source of life and the origin of all beings, the beginning of everything! This flame brings everything into existence, and nothing is destroyed except by its consuming fire. It reveals itself by its own nature. This fire cannot be contained in any place, for it has no physical form and no material substance. It surrounds the heavens entirely. From it, tiny sparks emerge, creating all the fires of the Sun, the Moon, and the Stars. This is what I understand about God. Do not seek to know more, for no matter how wise you are, it is beyond human comprehension. Know this: unjust and wicked people cannot hide from God's presence! No clever trick or excuse can conceal anything from His all-seeing eyes. God is present in everything, and everything is filled with God!

2. Within God is a vast depth of flame! Yet, the heart should not fear approaching this sacred fire or being touched by it. It is a gentle fire that will not destroy you. Its calm and soothing heat binds everything together, bringing harmony and stability to the world. Nothing exists without this fire, for it is God Himself. He has no creator and no mother. He knows all things and cannot be taught anything. His plans are perfect, and His name is beyond words. This is what God is! As for us, His messengers, we are only a small part of God.

Coelum Philosophorum

Paracelsus

Part I.

Concerning The Nature And Proper- Ties of Mercury

All things are hidden within everything. One thing among them acts as the container for the rest—their physical, visible, and moveable vessel. This vessel reveals all processes of melting or liquefying. It is a living, physical spirit, and when it holds something solid or frozen inside it, those things become restless, wanting to escape. There is no proper name for this process of liquefaction, nor for where it originates. Since no natural heat can match it, it is compared to the fire of Gehenna. This kind of liquefaction is entirely different from those caused by ordinary heat or solidified by cold. Such weak transformations have no effect on Mercury, who rejects them altogether.

From this, we understand that earthly elements, in their destructive processes, cannot add to or take away from celestial powers, which are known as Quintessence or its elements. These higher forces are beyond the influence of earthly elements and cannot be controlled by them. Celestial and infernal forces do not obey the four basic elements—dry, moist, hot, or cold. None of these elements can act against a Quintessence. Each higher power holds its own abilities and operates independently, without needing to rely on the elements.

Concerning The Nature and Proper- Ties of Jupiter

Within what is visible—specifically, the body of Jupiter—the other six physical metals are spiritually hidden, though each one is concealed with varying degrees of depth and strength. Jupiter does not contain any Quintessence in its makeup but consists of the four basic elements. Because of this, it melts under moderate heat and solidifies under moderate cold. Jupiter has a natural connection with the melting processes of all other metals. The more it resembles another metal, the easier it is for them to join together. Similar things interact more smoothly and naturally than those that are very different. Something distant will not affect or influence something else strongly. Similarly, distant things are neither feared nor desired, no matter how powerful they might be.

This explains why people do not strive to reach higher realms of creation—they seem too far away, and their greatness is beyond human understanding. Likewise, lower realms are not feared, since people are distant from them and unaware of the suffering they contain. Because of this, spirits from the underworld are considered insignificant. The farther away something is, the less valuable it appears, while things close to us are given more importance. Each thing changes based on its place, becoming better or transforming according to where it belongs, as shown by many examples.

Jupiter is farther away from Mars and Venus but closer to the Sun (Sol) and Moon (Luna). Because of this, Jupiter contains more qualities similar to gold and silver. The closer it is to Sol and Luna, the more beautiful, powerful, visible, and valuable it becomes—far more so than a distant object. On the other hand, the farther something is, the less value it seems to hold, and things nearby are always favored over distant ones. As something nearby becomes clearer, what is farther away becomes hidden. As an alchemist, you must seriously consider how you can move Jupiter to a distant place occupied by Sol and Luna and bring Sol and Luna closer to where Jupiter is now. The goal is to have Sol and Luna present before your eyes in their full physical forms, just as Jupiter is.

There are practical methods for changing metals from imperfection to perfection. First, mix the metals together. Then, separate the pure parts from the impure. This process is simply one of transformation, carefully guided by proper alchemical work. Take note that Jupiter contains a significant amount of gold and some silver. If you combine it with Saturn and Luna, Luna will increase in its presence and strength.

Concerning Mars and His Properties

The six hidden metals have cast out the seventh, making it solid and giving it little power while making it heavy and hard. In doing so, they have transferred their own hardness and ability to solidify into this new body. However, they have kept their color, ability to melt, and noble qualities for themselves.

It is difficult and takes great effort to turn an ordinary man into a prince or king. But Mars, with a strong and aggressive nature, takes control and seizes the throne. Even so, he must stay alert, guarding against unexpected traps that could capture him off-guard. It is also important to consider how Mars can rise to power and take the place of the king, while Sol, Luna, and Saturn take over the role that Mars once held.

Concerning Venus and Its Properties

The other six metals have transformed Venus into an external body by giving it their color and melting properties. To fully understand this, we should use some examples to show how something obvious can become hidden, and how something hidden can be made physically visible through the use of fire. Anything that can burn can naturally change its form through fire, turning into lime, soot, ash, glass, colors, stone, or earth. This earth can, in turn, be reshaped into new metallic bodies.

If a metal is burned or weakened by rust, it can regain its flexibility and strength through the careful application of fire.

Concerning The Nature And Proper- Ties op Saturn

Saturn speaks of himself in this way: "The other six metals have cast me out as their examiner. They have pushed me away from their spiritual state and given me a physical, perishable body as my dwelling, making me into something they are not and have no desire to become. My six brothers are spiritual in nature, and whenever I am placed in the fire, they enter my body and are destroyed along with me—except for Sol and Luna. These two are purified and made more noble by my waters. My spirit is like water, softening the rigid and frozen bodies of my brothers. However, my body is drawn toward the earth, and anything that enters into me takes on the same nature, becoming part of a single unified body through us.

It would do the world little good to know, or even believe, what lies hidden within me and what I am capable of achieving. It would be more valuable for the world to discover what I can do with myself. By abandoning the complex methods of the alchemists and focusing only on what I possess within me, people could find what I am truly able to accomplish. Within me lies the cold stone, a type of water that causes the spirits of the six metals to freeze together, creating the essence of the seventh metal. This process supports the transformation of Sol and Luna."

There are two types of antimony. One is the common black variety, which purifies Sol when it is melted within it. This black antimony has the closest connection to Saturn. The second type is white and is also known as magnesia or bismuth. It shares a strong connection with Jupiter, and when mixed with the black antimony, it increases the power of Luna.

Concerning Luna And The Properties Thereof

The attempt to transform Luna into Saturn or Mars is no easier than turning Mercury, Jupiter, Mars, Venus, or Saturn into Luna with great success. It is not useful to change something perfect into something imperfect; instead, the goal is to transform the imperfect into the perfect. Still, it is important to understand what Luna is made of and where it originates. Anyone who cannot figure this out will not be able to create Luna.

So, what exactly is Luna? It is one of the seven metals, standing as the seventh. It exists externally as a physical, material substance, but within it, the other six metals are spiritually hidden. These six spiritual metals cannot exist on their own without a physical metal to contain them. Similarly, a physical metal cannot exist without these six spiritual elements. All seven metals can mix easily when melted together, but this kind of mixture is not enough to create Sol or Luna. Even when combined, each metal retains its own nature—either remaining stable in the fire or being burned away by it.

For example, if you mix Mercury, Jupiter, Saturn, Mars, Venus, Sol, and Luna into a single mass, the result will not be a transformation of the other metals into Sol or Luna. Even though they all melt together, each keeps its own essence. This is how physical mixtures work. However, when it comes to the spiritual mixture and unity of metals, it is important to understand that no separation or destruction of the spirit is truly possible. Spiritual elements cannot exist without physical bodies. Even if a body is destroyed and transformed a hundred times, the spirit within will always gain a new, more noble form. This process is the transformation of metals from one level to another—moving from a lesser form to a higher one, such as Luna. From there, the metal can be perfected into Sol, the brightest and most royal of all metals.

It is true, as mentioned before, that the six metals will always generate a seventh from within themselves, revealing it clearly in its true form.

One might ask: If Luna, like all metals, comes from the other six, what are its properties and nature? The answer is that no other metal besides Luna can be formed from the combination of Saturn, Mercury, Jupiter, Mars, Venus, and Sol. Each of these metals contributes two key qualities to Luna, making a total of twelve virtues. These twelve virtues represent the spirit of Luna, and each metal offers something unique to its composition.

Luna gains liquidity and its bright white color from Mercury, along with influences from the zodiac signs Aquarius and Pisces. It receives its whiteness and resistance to fire from Jupiter, along with traits from Sagittarius and Taurus. From Mars, along with Cancer and Aries, Luna gets its hardness and clear, ringing sound. From Venus, along with Gemini and Libra, Luna gains the ability to solidify. From Saturn, along with Virgo and Scorpio, Luna inherits a consistent body and weight. Finally, from Sol, with influences from Leo and Virgo, Luna receives its pure, spotless nature and strong resistance to fire.

This is the essence of Luna's spiritual and physical qualities. It is a combination of the six metals and their virtues, reflecting both wisdom and the natural order of exaltation, briefly summarized for understanding.

It is also important to explain what kind of body metallic spirits take on during their initial creation through the influence of the heavens. When a miner crushes a seemingly worthless stone, he melts it down, corrupts it, and completely breaks it apart with fire. During this process of destruction, the metallic spirit takes on a new body— one that is stronger and more refined. Instead of being brittle, it becomes soft and flexible.

Then the alchemist steps in, further corrupting, breaking down, and carefully refining this metallic body. Through this process, the spirit within the metal takes on an even more perfect form, revealing itself more clearly—unless it is Sol or Luna, which are already perfected. At last, the spirit and the body of the metal become fully united. They are now protected from the effects of ordinary fire and have reached a state where they cannot be corrupted.

Concerning The Nature of Sol And Its Properties

The seventh metal, after the six spiritual ones, is Sol, which is purely fire in its nature. Outwardly, it is the most beautiful, brilliant, clear, and noticeable of all metals. It also has the heaviest and most uniform body. This is because it holds within itself the frozen essence of the other six metals, combining them into one solid form. Sol's ability to melt comes from either the heat of fire or the hidden influence of Mercury, along with the zodiac signs Pisces and Aquarius, that exist spiritually within it. We can see proof of this because Mercury blends effortlessly with Sol, almost as if in an embrace.

However, after Sol melts and the fire's heat is removed, cold takes over, causing it to harden. To make Sol solid and stable, it requires the essence of the other five metals—Jupiter, Saturn, Mars, Venus, and Luna—each of which contributes its cold nature. Because of this, Sol is difficult to keep in liquid form without the constant heat of fire. Mercury cannot provide enough heat on its own to keep Sol melted, nor can it resist the coldness of the other five metals. Mercury's natural role is simply to stay in liquid form and flow, not to harden or make anything solid.

Heat and life belong to the same nature, bringing movement and fluidity, while cold brings hardness, stillness, and the absence of life, which can be compared to death. For instance, the six cold metals—Jupiter, Saturn, Mars, Venus, Luna, and even Venus again—can only be melted by the heat of fire. Snow and ice, being cold, will only cause things to harden further. Once a metal melted by fire cools, the cold seizes it, making it solid and frozen in place.

As for Mercury, in order to remain fluid and full of life, it depends on heat, not cold. Anyone who claims Mercury lives through cold and moisture misunderstands nature and follows common but mistaken beliefs. The truth is that life comes from warmth and fire, while cold brings death. Sol's fire is pure—it is not a living fire, but it is solid and contains the colors of sulfur, a perfect blend of yellow and red.

The five cold metals—Jupiter, Mars, Saturn, Venus, and Luna—each give Sol part of their nature. They contribute solidity through coldness, color through fire, hardness through dryness, weight through moisture, and sound through brightness. Gold, which is Sol's material form, cannot be burned or destroyed by ordinary earthly fire. This is because one fire cannot burn another fire; instead, adding fire to fire only makes it stronger.

The celestial fire we receive from the Sun on Earth is not the same as the fire in heaven or the fire we know on Earth. The fire from the Sun, when it reaches us, becomes cold and frozen—it forms the body of the Sun as we experience it. Therefore, earthly fire cannot overcome the fire of the Sun. Instead, the Sun's celestial fire melts objects, like snow or ice, but is never burned itself. Fire does not have the power to burn fire, because Sol is fire—its essence dissolved in the heavens but solidified here on Earth.

Gold is in its
1 Celestial
Dissolved Essence three
2 Elementary} and Fluid fold
3 Metallic is Corporeal.

Part II

God and Nature Do Nothing in Vain

The eternal nature of all things, existing beyond time, with no beginning or end, is always at work. It operates even in places where no hope can be found. It accomplishes what seems impossible. What once appeared beyond belief or hope reveals itself as truth in a marvelous and unexpected way.

Note on Mercurius Vivus

Whatever gives a white color carries the essence of life and the qualities of light, which naturally bring life into being. In contrast, anything that produces blackness shares the nature of death, carrying the qualities of darkness and the forces that lead to death. The earth, with its cold nature, symbolizes this hardness, as it solidifies and fixes things. A house, for example, is always lifeless, but the person who lives inside it is alive. If you can understand the power of this idea, you have gained mastery.

Tested liquefactive powder: Burn the fat of verbena.

Recipe: Four ounces of saltpeter, half as much sulfur, and one ounce of tartar. Mix them and melt.

What Is to Be Thought Concerning The Congelation Of Mercury

Trying to solidify Mercury and turn it into Luna, while also refining it through great effort, is a waste of time. This process only leads to the loss of the Sol and Luna already present within Mercury. There is a much simpler and quicker way to transform Mercury into Luna, without the need for freezing or excessive labor. This method minimizes waste and saves effort, making it possible to create silver and gold with ease.

Anyone can learn this alchemical process since it is straightforward and simple. By using it, one can produce large amounts of silver and gold in a short time. Long, complicated explanations are unnecessary—most people prefer clear instructions. So, follow these steps, and you will create Sol and Luna, which will bring you wealth. Pay close attention as I explain this process briefly. Keep these instructions well in mind so that, by working with Saturn, Mercury, and Jupiter, you can produce Sol and Luna.

There is no easier or more effective method in alchemy, and it requires very little effort to master. The process for making Sol and Luna is so fast that no further books or detailed lessons are needed— writing more about it would be as pointless as documenting last year's snow.

Concerning The Receipts of Alchemy

What, then, should we say about the recipes used in alchemy, along with the many different tools and vessels? These include furnaces, glassware, jars, waters, oils, lime, sulfur, salts, saltpeter, alum, vitriol, chrysocolla, copper greens, black inks, orpiment, green vitriol, white lead, red earth, thucia, wax, lutum sapientiae (the clay of wisdom), ground glass, verdigris, soot, eggshells, crocus of Mars, soap, crystal, chalk, arsenic, antimony, red lead, elixirs, lazurite, gold leaf, sal ammoniac, calamine stone, magnesia, Armenian bole, and many other substances.

Moreover, the steps involved—such as fermentation, digestion, testing, dissolving, cementing, filtering, refining, burning, distilling, purifying, and more—fill alchemical books to the brim. Then there are the materials drawn from herbs, roots, seeds, woods, stones, animals, worms, bone dust, snail shells, other shells, and pitch. Many of these things, however, only make the work more complicated. Even if Sol and Luna could be made with them, they would slow down the process rather than help it. The truth is that the art of creating Sol and Luna is not learned from these things. Therefore, they can be ignored, as they do not help when working with the five metals to make Sol and Luna.

Someone might ask, "What is the quick and easy way to create Sol and Luna, without unnecessary effort?" The answer is that this process has already been explained clearly and thoroughly in the Seven Canons. There is no point in trying to teach it to someone who does not grasp these Canons, as it would be difficult to convince them that this knowledge can be understood, though it must be approached in a hidden way rather than openly.

The art is this: Once you have created heaven, or the sphere of Saturn, and allowed its life to flow across the earth, place upon it the planets—whichever ones you choose—ensuring that Luna plays the smallest role. Let them run their course until Saturn, or heaven, has vanished entirely. At that point, the planets will remain lifeless, with their old, corruptible forms discarded. However, they will have gained new, perfect, and incorruptible bodies.

These new bodies are the spirit of heaven. From this spirit, the planets receive new forms and life, and they continue as they did before. Take this body, born from both life and earth, and keep it. It is Sol and Luna. Here, then, is the entire art, explained plainly and completely. If you still do not understand it, or have not practiced it, that is fine. It is better that this knowledge remains hidden and not revealed to everyone.

How To Conjure The Crystal So That All Things May Be Seen In It

To conjure means nothing more than to observe something correctly, to know what it is, and to fully understand it. A crystal is a representation of the air. Whatever appears in the air—whether it moves or stays still—also appears as a reflection or wave within the crystal or mirror. This is because air, water, and crystal are the same in terms of how we see through them. They function like a mirror, showing a reversed image of whatever is reflected within them.

Concerning The Heat of Mercury

Those who believe that Mercury is naturally cold and moist are mistaken. In truth, Mercury is warm and moist by nature, which is why it remains in a constant state of fluidity. If it were cold and moist, it would behave like frozen water, always solid and hard, requiring fire to melt it, as is the case with other metals. But Mercury doesn't need fire to become liquid. Its own natural heat keeps it fluid, giving it the ability to move freely, or "quick," meaning it cannot be killed, solidified, or frozen.

It is important to note that when the spirits of the seven metals, or however many are combined, meet fire, they compete with one another—especially Mercury. Each metal tries to display its powers and virtues, working to dominate the others through liquefaction and transformation. One metal will take on the life and properties of another, giving a new form and nature to the one it overtakes. The heat stirs the spirits or vapors of the metals to interact with each other, constantly changing one into another until they reach perfection and purity.

What, then, must be done to Mercury to remove its natural warmth and moisture, and replace them with extreme cold that will solidify, bind, and fully harden it? Follow this method: Take pure Mercury and seal it tightly in a silver container. Place this container in the middle of a jar filled with pieces of lead. Allow it to melt for twenty-four hours, or one full day. This process removes Mercury's hidden heat, adds external warmth, and introduces the coldness of Saturn and Luna, two planets with cold properties. This forces Mercury to freeze, solidify, and become firm.

It is important to understand that the cold needed to solidify Mercury is not the same as the cold we feel from snow or ice. Instead, this cold has a different quality—on the surface, there may even seem to be some warmth. Likewise, the heat that keeps Mercury fluid is not the same kind of heat we normally experience. Instead, Mercury can feel cool to the touch, which has led some scholars, who speak more than they understand, to wrongly conclude that Mercury is cold and moist. They mistakenly suggest that heat will solidify Mercury, but instead, heat makes it even more fluid, as they continue to discover at their own expense.

True alchemy, which teaches the only way to make Sol and Luna from the five imperfect metals, offers this principle: "Only from metals, within metals, by metals, and through metals can perfect metals be made." In some metals lies the essence of Luna, and in others, the essence of Sol.

What Materials And Instruments Are Required in Alchemy

All you need are a foundry, bellows, tongs, hammers, cauldrons, jars, and small refining dishes made from beech ashes. After gathering these tools, introduce the metals—Saturn, Jupiter, Mars, Sol, Venus, Mercury, and Luna. Let the process run its course, finishing with Saturn.

The Method of Seeking Minerals

The hope of finding metals within the earth and stones is very uncertain, and the effort required is immense. However, since this is the most direct way to obtain them, it should not be dismissed but highly praised. This desire to seek metals should be encouraged, just as the natural desire for marriage in youth and adulthood is accepted.

Just as bees are drawn to roses and other flowers to create honey and wax, so too should people—apart from greed or selfish ambition—seek metals within the earth. Whoever does not search for them is unlikely to find them. God grants not only gold and silver to some but also poverty, hardship, and suffering.

Some people, however, are given special knowledge of metals and minerals, enabling them to discover easier ways to create gold and silver. These methods are faster than digging and smelting, allowing them to extract precious metals from their original forms. This applies not only to things found underground but also to metals refined from imperfect minerals. Gold and silver (Sol and Luna) can be made from any of the five metals—Mercury, Jupiter, Saturn, Mars, and Venus—although some are easier to work with than others. Sol and Luna can be made more easily from Mercury, Saturn, and Jupiter, while it is more difficult to create them from Mars and Venus, though it is still possible with the addition of existing Sol and Luna. For example, Luna can be produced from Magnesium and Saturn, while pure Sol can be made from Jupiter and Cinnabar.

A skilled alchemist, through careful thought and study, can perfect the transformation of metals better than by relying on the movements of the twelve zodiac signs or the seven planets. It is unnecessary to follow these celestial movements, whether they indicate favorable or unfavorable days, good or bad planetary influences. These things neither help nor hinder the process of natural alchemy. If you have a working process, you can perform the operation whenever you choose. However, if something is missing from your method or understanding, no alignment of stars or planets will make up for it.

Metals that remain buried in the earth for too long not only rust but can also transform into natural stones over time, though this is known to very few. In fact, old coins from ancient times, bearing various images, are sometimes found in the earth. These coins were originally made of metal but, through the slow transformation of nature, have turned into stone.

What Alchemy Is

Alchemy is the deliberate effort to change one type of metal into another. Each person, using their own understanding, can find the best path and discover the truth, as truth is revealed to those who pursue it with dedication. It is essential to understand both stars and stones because the spirit of all stones is linked to the stars. Sol (the Sun) and Luna (the Moon), representing celestial bodies, are also connected to a single stone. The stones of the earth originate from these celestial stones. Through fire, purification, and separation, these earthly stones are made bright and pure, much like their celestial counterparts. The entire earth is made from a mixture of materials that have solidified into a stony mass resting within the larger sphere of the universe.

Precious stones found on earth are the closest in perfection to the heavenly stones. These earthly stones possess purity, beauty, brilliance, strength, and resistance to fire, just like celestial stones. However, they are often found in rough environments, and most people mistakenly believe these stones were created exactly where they were found. They assume that these stones were simply polished and traded for their beauty, color, and value. A brief description of these stones follows:

The Emerald is a transparent green stone. It is said to improve eyesight and memory and protect purity. If the person carrying it loses their purity, the stone will lose its perfection.

The Adamant is a black crystal, also called Evax, known for bringing joy to those who carry it. It is dark, with a metallic color, and is the hardest of all stones. However, it can dissolve in goat's blood. It rarely grows larger than a hazelnut.

The Magnet is a stone made of iron that attracts iron to itself.

The Pearl is not truly a stone since it forms inside seashells. It is white and grows within living creatures, like fish or mollusks, which makes it different from typical stones.

The Jacinth is a yellow, transparent stone. Its name also refers to a flower, which legend says was once a man.

The Sapphire is a stone with a heavenly color and is considered connected to celestial qualities.

The Ruby glows with an intense red color.

The Carbuncle is a solar stone that shines as brightly as the sun itself.

The Coral is a stone that can be white or red. It forms in the sea, growing like a plant or shrub. When exposed to air, it hardens and becomes fireproof.

The Chalcedony is a stone with mixed colors, sitting between transparency and opacity, often with cloudy or liver-colored patterns. It is considered the least valuable of the precious stones.

The Topaz is known to shine at night and is found among rocks.

The Amethyst is a stone with a purple or blood-red hue.

The Chrysoprasus shines like fire at night and resembles gold during the day.

The Crystal is a transparent white stone that looks like ice. It forms from the essence of other stones through extraction and purification.

The key to understanding these stones lies in knowing their origins and connection to metals. The truth is that metals are the most refined part of common stones. They contain elements like oil, fat, and grease, but they remain impure and imperfect as long as they are mixed within the stones. To create perfect metals, these elements must be identified, separated, and extracted from the stones through a process of melting and refining. Once purified, the substance becomes a metal comparable to the stars, which are themselves like separated stones from the heavens.

Those who study metals and minerals must be guided by reason and intelligence. They should not limit themselves to exploring only the known metals buried deep within mountains. Often, valuable metals are found closer to the earth's surface, while deeper layers may not yield the same quality. Every stone—whether a large boulder or a simple rock—must be examined carefully, for even a stone that seems worthless might contain hidden value, sometimes more valuable than livestock. The place where a stone is found does not always determine its true worth, as the influence of the sky plays a role in its formation. Even common earth, dust, or sand can contain traces of gold or silver, and those who look carefully will notice this.

The Emerald Tablet

(Thoth the Atlantean)

Hermes Trismegistus

The Emerald Tablets Of
Thoth The Atlantean

The story behind these tablets is unusual and may seem unbelievable to modern scientists. They are said to be incredibly ancient, going back around 36,000 years before the common era. The author is Thoth, an Atlantean priest-king, who established a colony in Egypt after the destruction of Atlantis.

Thoth is credited with building the Great Pyramid of Giza, though it has been wrongly attributed to Cheops. In the pyramid, he stored his knowledge and preserved the records and tools from ancient Atlantis. Thoth ruled over Egypt for about 16,000 years, from around 52,000 to 36,000 BCE. Under his leadership, the once primitive people of Egypt rose to a high level of civilization.

Thoth had overcome death and could pass from life only when he chose, without actually dying. His great wisdom made him ruler over many Atlantean colonies, including those in South and Central America. When it was time for him to leave Egypt, he built the Great Pyramid over the entrance to the Halls of Amenti, where he placed his records and selected the most worthy people to guard his secrets.

In later times, these guardians became the priests of the pyramids, and Thoth was worshiped as a god of wisdom and the Recorder. In the age that followed his departure, the Halls of Amenti became known in legend as the underworld, where souls went after death for judgment.

Thoth's spirit continued to incarnate in human form, as described in the tablets. He returned three times, with his last appearance as Hermes, known as the "thrice-born." During this incarnation, he left behind writings known as the Emerald Tablets, a later and more simplified version of the ancient mysteries.

The tablets translated in this work are ten in total, originally placed in the Great Pyramid under the care of the pyramid priests. For convenience, the content has been divided into thirteen sections. The final two tablets contain such powerful knowledge that it is currently forbidden to release them to the public. However, the ones included here hold valuable secrets for those who are serious about seeking wisdom. They should not be read just once but studied many times, as only through careful reading can their deeper meanings be understood. A casual reading will provide glimpses of beauty, but true insight comes only through deep study.

Now, let me explain how these ancient secrets were brought back to light after being hidden for so long. Around 1,300 BCE, Egypt was in turmoil, and many priests were sent to other parts of the world. Among them were some of the pyramid priests carrying the Emerald Tablets. They used the tablets as a symbol of authority, allowing them to influence less advanced priesthoods in other regions descended from Atlantean colonies.

These priests eventually settled in South America, where they found the Mayan civilization, which had preserved much of the ancient wisdom. The priests stayed with the Mayans, and by the 10th century, the Mayan people had established themselves in the Yucatan. The Emerald Tablets were placed under the altar of a great Sun Temple.

After the Spanish conquest, the Mayan cities were abandoned, and the treasures within their temples were forgotten. It's important to understand that the Great Pyramid has always been a temple for initiation into the mysteries. Even figures like Jesus, Solomon, and Apollonius were initiated there.

The author of this translation, who is connected to the Great White Lodge that works through the pyramid priesthood, was instructed to retrieve the tablets and return them to the Great Pyramid. After many adventures, the tablets were recovered. Before returning them, permission was granted to translate and keep a copy of the wisdom they contain. This translation was completed in 1925, and only now has permission been given to release part of it to the public.

Some people will doubt its authenticity, but true seekers will find wisdom within these words. If the light is already within you, the light in these tablets will resonate with your soul.

Now, let me describe the physical nature of the tablets. They are made of a bright emerald-green material, created through a process of alchemical transformation. These tablets are imperishable and immune to all natural elements, with their atomic structure remaining stable forever. In this way, they defy the natural laws of matter and ionization.

The ancient Atlantean language is engraved on their surfaces, and these inscriptions respond to focused thoughts, releasing mental vibrations that awaken understanding in the reader. The tablets are held together by hoops of a golden-colored alloy, suspended from a rod made of the same material.

The knowledge within these tablets forms the foundation of the ancient mysteries. Anyone who reads them with an open mind will greatly expand their wisdom. Read them, believe or not, but read them—and the vibrations within will awaken a response in your soul.

In the following pages, I will reveal some of the deeper mysteries hinted at in previous writings. Humanity's search for the laws that govern life has been constant, but the truth has always been hidden just beyond the veil that separates the higher realms from the material world. Those who seek knowledge must learn to look inward, for the answers lie in silence, beyond the distractions of the physical senses. Those who talk do not know, and those who know do not speak.

The highest truths cannot be spoken, for they exist beyond words and symbols. Symbols serve as keys to understanding deeper truths, but often people cannot see what lies beyond the symbols because they seem too overwhelming. If we realize that all material symbols are just representations of higher truths, we begin to develop the vision to see beyond the veil.

Everything in the universe moves according to law. The laws that govern the planets are no different from the laws that shape human life. One of the most important Cosmic Laws is the one that connects the material aspect of humanity with the spiritual. The key to this connection lies in the intellectual part of human nature, which bridges the material and spiritual worlds.

Those who seek higher knowledge must strengthen their minds and concentrate all their energy on their chosen path. The search for light, life, and love begins on the material plane, but it reaches its ultimate goal in complete unity with the universal consciousness. The material world is only the starting point; the true goal is spiritual enlightenment.

In the following pages, I will interpret the Emerald Tablets and reveal some of their hidden meanings. The words of Thoth contain many layers of truth, and these hidden meanings will become clear with thoughtful reflection. If your own inner light is awakened, the knowledge within these tablets will resonate with your soul.

TABLET 1 I, Thoth, the Atlantean, master of ancient mysteries, keeper of sacred knowledge, and mighty ruler, have lived through countless generations. As I prepare to enter the Halls of Amenti, I write down this wisdom for those who come after me. In the great city of Keor, on the island of Undal, I began this life long ago. The people of Atlantis were not like the men of today—they did not live short lives, but instead, they renewed their existence over and over through the Halls of Amenti, where the river of life flows eternally.

I have traveled down the dark path that leads to light a hundred times over, and just as many times I have returned from darkness, renewed in strength and power. Now, I leave once more, and the people of Khem (ancient Egypt) will no longer see me. But one day, I will rise again, mighty and powerful, to demand an account from those I left behind. Beware, people of Khem, if you have betrayed my teachings, for I will cast you down into the darkness from which you came.

Do not reveal my secrets to those from the North or the South, or my curse will fall upon you. Remember my words, for I will return and demand from you all that you have been entrusted with. Even from beyond time and death, I will return to reward or punish you according to how you have followed my truths.

My people were great in ancient times, far greater than the people who live now. We held knowledge that reached into the depths of the universe, uncovering wisdom from Earth's earliest days. We were wise with the knowledge of the Children of Light, who lived among us, and we drew power from the eternal fire. Among us, the greatest of all men was my father, Thotme, the keeper of the great temple and the link between the Children of Light and the people who lived across the ten islands of Atlantis. He was the voice of the Dweller of Unal, whose words the kings obeyed.

I grew up under my father's guidance, learning the ancient mysteries, and the fire of wisdom grew within me until it consumed my soul. On a great day, the Dweller of the Temple summoned me before him. Few men had looked upon his face and lived, for the Children of Light, when not in physical form, are not like the sons of men. I was chosen from among humanity to be taught by the Dweller, so that I might carry out his purposes, which were not yet born in the world.

For long ages, I lived in the temple, learning ever more wisdom until I reached the light of the great fire. The Dweller taught me the path to Amenti, the underworld where the great king sits on his throne of power. I bowed before the Lords of Life and Death, and they gave me the Key of Life. I was freed from the cycle of death and rebirth. I traveled to the stars, where space and time meant nothing, and after drinking deeply from the cup of wisdom, I looked into the hearts of men. There, I discovered even greater mysteries, and my soul was at peace.

Throughout the ages, I have watched people die and be reborn in the light of life. But as Atlantis declined, the consciousness that had once been one with me faded, replaced by lesser beings from distant stars. Following the laws of the universe, the word of the Master began to take form. The thoughts of the Atlanteans turned downward into darkness, and the Dweller awoke from his detachment, calling forth his power. Deep in the heart of the Earth, the Sons of Amenti heard his call. Using the power of the Logos, they directed the eternal fire, shifting its course.

A great flood swept over the world, shifting the balance of the Earth, and only the Temple of Light remained standing on the mountain of Undal, still rising above the water. Some among us survived the flood. The Master commanded me to gather my people and take them across the waters to the land of the barbarians who lived in caves. There, we would carry out the plan we knew so well.

I gathered my people, and we boarded the Master's great ship. As we rose into the morning sky, the Temple of Light disappeared beneath the rising waters. It vanished from the Earth until the appointed time when it would return. We fled toward the rising sun, and beneath us lay the land of the children of Khem. When we arrived, the barbarians came at us with spears and clubs, filled with rage and intent on destroying the Sons of Atlantis.

I raised my staff and directed a ray of vibration at them, freezing them in place like stones from the mountain. Then I spoke to them calmly, telling them of the greatness of Atlantis and explaining that we were messengers of the Sun. I used my knowledge of magic and science to subdue them until they bowed before me. When I released them, they groveled at my feet in fear.

We lived in the land of Khem for many long years. Following the Master's command, I eventually sent the Sons of Atlantis to distant lands, so that the wisdom of Atlantis could rise again in the future. Through the womb of time, knowledge would once more be reborn in those who seek it.

For a long time, I lived in the land of Khem, using my knowledge to perform great works. The people of Khem grew in understanding, nourished by the wisdom I shared. To retain my power, I opened a path to Amenti, allowing me to live through the ages as a Sun of Atlantis, preserving knowledge and records. The people of Khem became strong, conquering those around them and slowly rising in spiritual strength.

Now I must leave them and descend into the dark halls of Amenti, deep within the Earth, where I will stand once more before the Dweller. Above the entrance to Amenti, I raised a gateway—only a few have the courage to cross it. Over the portal, I built a mighty pyramid, harnessing the power that defies Earth's gravity. Inside, I placed a force-chamber, creating a circular passage that reaches near the top. At the summit, I set a crystal to send a ray through time and space, drawing energy from the ether and focusing it toward the gateway of Amenti.

I built other chambers that seem empty but hide the keys to Amenti within them. Only those who dare to explore the dark realms may enter, but first, they must purify themselves through fasting. Those who seek the mysteries must lie in the stone sarcophagus within my chamber, and then the hidden truths will be revealed. Even in the depths of the Earth, I will meet them. I, Thoth, the Lord of Wisdom, will dwell with them always.

I built the Great Pyramid, designing it to align with the forces of the Earth, so it would burn with energy for eternity and stand through the ages. Inside, I placed my knowledge of magic and science, ensuring I could return from Amenti. While my body sleeps in the halls, my soul will roam freely, incarnating among humans in different forms, including as Hermes, thrice-born.

I serve as the Dweller's messenger on Earth, following his commands to guide many toward enlightenment. Now I return to the halls of Amenti, leaving behind fragments of my wisdom. Keep the Dweller's command: Always lift your gaze toward the light. In time, you will become one with the Master, united with the All. I leave now, but remember my teachings. Live by them, and I will be with you, guiding you into the light. As the portal opens before me, I descend into the night's darkness.

Deep in the heart of the Earth lie the Halls of Amenti, beneath the sunken islands of Atlantis. These halls are places for both the living and the dead, illuminated by the fire of the infinite All. In a distant past, the Children of Light observed humanity's struggle, seeing that people were bound by forces beyond them. They knew that only by breaking free could humans rise from Earth toward the Sun. The Children of Light took human form and came down to Earth, saying, "We are beings formed from the dust of space, part of the infinite All. Though we live as humans, we are not entirely like them."

They created vast spaces beneath the Earth's surface, far from where humans lived, surrounding these halls with powerful forces to protect them from harm. They built other spaces nearby, filling them with life and light from above. In these hidden places, they built the Halls of Amenti to dwell there eternally, living with endless life.

Thirty-two of the Children of Light came among humans, seeking to free them from the darkness and the forces that bound them. In the Halls of Life, a bright, flaming flower grew, expanding and driving away the darkness. At its center, they placed a powerful ray, filling all who came near with life and light. Around the flower, they arranged thirty-two thrones, where the Children of Light sat, bathed in its radiance and filled with the eternal light.

Over the ages, they placed their original bodies in these halls, reawakening them every thousand years with the life-giving light, which quickened their spirits. Though they appeared to sleep, their souls moved freely through the bodies of men, guiding and teaching them. As their bodies rested, they incarnated among humans, leading them from darkness into the light. In the Halls of Life, they kept knowledge unknown to humanity, living forever beneath the cool fire of life.

At times, they awakened from their rest, coming forth as lights among people, infinite beings among finite men. Those who rise from darkness into light are freed from the Halls of Amenti and the Flower of Life. With wisdom as their guide, they pass from among men to join the Masters of Life, free from the bonds of darkness. In the center of the radiant flower sit seven Lords from realms beyond time, guiding humanity with infinite wisdom along the path through time. Though they are silent and hidden, their power is immense, and their knowledge is endless.

Drawing from the Life force, different yet connected to the children of men. Though different, they are also One with the Children of Light. They guard and watch over the forces that bind humanity, ready to release them when the time for enlightenment arrives.

At the forefront sits the Veiled Presence, the Lord of Lords, the infinite Nine, standing above the Lords of the Cycles—Three, Four, Five, Six, Seven, and Eight—each with a purpose and unique power, guiding and shaping human destiny. They sit in strength and wisdom, untouched by time or space. Though not of this world, they are connected to it, like Elder Brothers to humanity. With wisdom, they judge and observe, watching how the Light grows within mankind.

The Dweller led me before them, and I witnessed him blend with the ONE from above. A voice came forth, saying, "Thoth, you are great among the children of men. From this moment, you are free from the Halls of Amenti, a Master of Life among men. Death will come to you only if you desire it. Drink from the well of Life for all eternity, for Life is now yours to take. Death is yours to command at will. Stay here or leave when you wish; Amenti is open to you, a Sun among men. Take Life in any form you choose, Child of the Light who has grown among humanity.

Though free, you must always labor along the path of Light. You have taken one step on the endless journey upward, but the mountain of Light stretches infinitely before you. Every step you take raises the mountain higher; each bit of progress makes the goal seem farther away. You will forever move toward infinite Wisdom, but the goal will always stay just out of reach. You are now free from the Halls of Amenti."

Thank You for Reading

Dear Reader,

We hope this timeless classic has sparked your imagination and enriched your literary journey. Now that you've turned the final page, we want to share a vision for the future of reading—one where every classic you've ever wanted to explore is at your fingertips, in a format that best suits your life.

We'd like to invite you to gain immediate, unlimited digital & audiobook access to hundreds of the most treasured literary classics ever written—along with the option to secure deluxe paperback, hardcover & box set editions at printing cost. Together, we can spark a new global literary renaissance alongside our small, independent publishing house called "The Library of Alexandria."

Thousands of years ago, the Library of Alexandria stood as a beacon of knowledge—until it was lost to history. We aim to reignite that spirit of preservation and discovery right now, in the modern age—only this time, it's accessible to all, in every language and every format.

Picture a world where every timeless classic, novel, poem, or philosophical treatise is not only available to read but also updated for today's readers—modernized, translated into any language or dialect, and ready to enjoy in any format you choose, whether that is in an eBook, audiobook, paperback, or deluxe hardcover & box set version a printing cost.

By joining our movement to rebuild the modern Library of Alexandria, you become part of an unprecedented mission to offer:

- **Unlimited Audiobook & eBook Access to the Greatest Classics of All Time**

  Instantly explore thousands of legendary works, from Plato and Shakespeare to Jane Austen and Leo Tolstoy. All are instantly ready to read or listen to, giving you a complete literary universe at your fingertips.

- **Paperback & Deluxe Editions at Printing Costs:**

  Purchase any title in a paperback, deluxe hardbound, or deluxe boxset edition at printing costs, shipped right to your doorstep. Curate your personal library of Alexandria with editions worthy of display—crafted to last, designed to captivate, and delivered straight to your door.

- **Modern translations for Contemporary Readers in all languages and dialects**

  Discover a vast selection of classics reimagined in clear, current language—no more struggling with outdated phrases or obscure references. Next to the original versions, we aim to offer translations in as many languages and dialects as possible.

  As we continue our translation efforts and add new languages, readers everywhere can connect with these works as if they were written today. By bridging linguistic divides, you're contributing to ensuring that these timeless stories become more meaningful, accessible, and inspiring for people across the globe.

- **Your Personal Library of Alexandria:**

  Over the months and years, you'll curate a unique physical archive of classics—each volume a testament to your taste, curiosity, and love of knowledge. It's not just about owning books—it's about curating a cultural legacy you'll cherish and pass down for generations to come.

- **Join a Global Literary Renaissance:**

  Your support fuels an ongoing mission: allowing us to reinvest in offering deluxe print editions (including special boxsets) at their true cost, broaden the range of available formats and translations, and extend the reach of these works to new audiences worldwide. By joining today, you're not just preserving a legacy of masterpieces; you set in motion a powerful wave of literary accessibility.

We are more than a publisher—we're a movement, and we can't do it alone. Your support lets us scale our mission, preserving and reimagining history's greatest works for tomorrow's readers.

Become a Torchbearer of knowledge.

Thank you for picking up this book and allowing us into your literary journey. As you turn the pages, know that you're part of something larger: a global effort to keep these stories alive, share their wisdom across borders and generations, and spark a true cultural revival for the modern era.

If this resonates with you—please consider taking the next step by visiting:

www.libraryofalexandria.com

With gratitude and a shared love of knowledge,

The Modern Library of Alexandria Team

Visit:

www.libraryofalexandria.com

Or scan the code below: